P9-DHA-658

Larry Gets Lost in San Francisco

Illustrated by John Skewes
Written by Michael Mullin and John Skewes

little bigfoot
an imprint of sasquatch books
seattle, wa

Manufactured in China by C&C Offset Printing Co. Ltd.
Shenzhen, Guangdong Province, in February 2015

Published by Little Bigfoot, an imprint of Sasquatch Books

20 19 18 17 16 15 12 11 10 9 8 7 6

Book design by Mint Design

Library of Congress Cataloging-in-Publication Data

Mullin, Michael.
Larry gets lost in San Francisco / illustrations by John Skewes ; written by Michael Mullin and John Skewes.
p. cm.
ISBN-13: 978-1-57061-567-2 (alk. paper)
ISBN-10: 1-57061-567-5 (alk. paper)
1. San Francisco (Calif.)--Juvenile literature. 2. San Francisco (Calif.)--Description and travel--Juvenile literature. 3. Historic buildings--California--San Francisco--Juvenile literature. 4. Historic sites--California--San Francisco--Juvenile literature. 5. San Francisco (Calif.)--Buildings, structures, etc.--Juvenile literature. I. Skewes, John. II. Title.
F869.S34M85 2009
979.4'61--dc22
2008039527

Larry adopts a food bank in every city he visits. A portion of the proceeds from this book will be donated to the San Francisco Food Bank. The Web site is www.sffoodbank.org.

SASQUATCH BOOKS
1904 Third Ave, Suite 710
Seattle, WA 98101
(206) 467-4300

www.sasquatchbooks.com
custserv@sasquatchbooks.com

This is **Larry.** This is **Pete.**
They like to ride in the back seat.

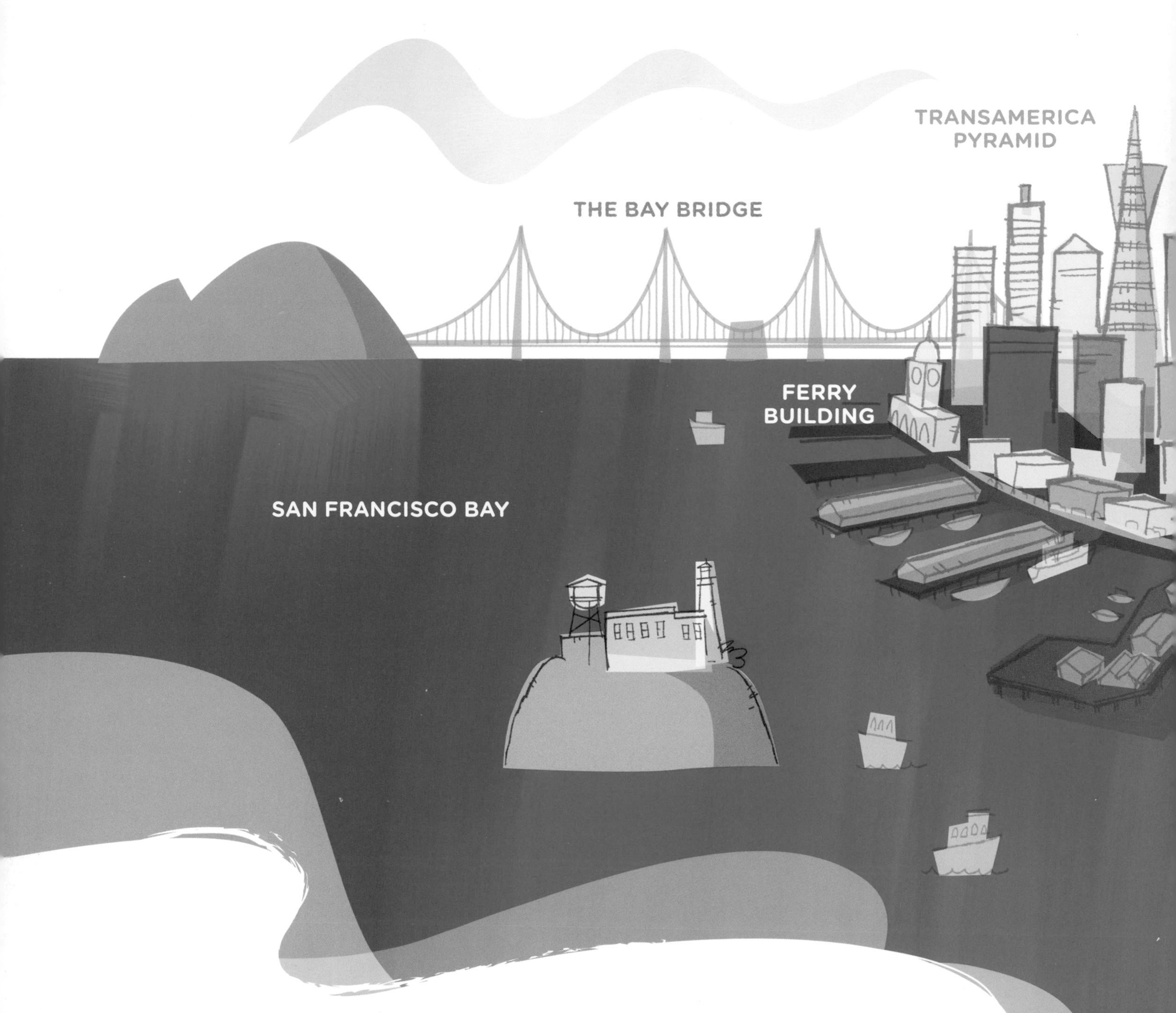

The car rolled along and soon broke through the fog,
Then Mom, Dad, Pete, and Larry, his dog,

Saw not one, but two bridges going their way.
One **reddish orange,** the other one **gray.**

GOLDEN GATE BRIDGE
Completed in 1937, the bridge is 746 feet tall and 8,981 feet long. It's painted a bright color so that it can be seen through the fog.

He first saw a building with a big yellow dome.
It looked like a place that a king might call home.

PALACE OF THE FINE ARTS
Turtles, ducks, and other water animals swim in the beautiful lagoon that surrounds this grand building.

GHIRARDELLI SQUARE (right)
There was once a big chocolate factory here, but now it is shops and restaurants. You can still buy all kinds of sweet treats to eat here. But remember, dogs can't eat chocolate!

The next place they saw
Was a beautiful square
With a scent
(Was that chocolate?)
That filled up the air.

From where Larry stood,
By the ground on all fours,
He saw an old wooden ship
Near the shore.

Pete's parents reminded them, **"Don't wander far"**
As they excitedly boarded a cable car.

These vehicles pulled along tracks on the ground
Are a popular way to get around town.

For the ride Larry sat himself right beside Pete
'Til he saw a glazed donut roll by down the street.

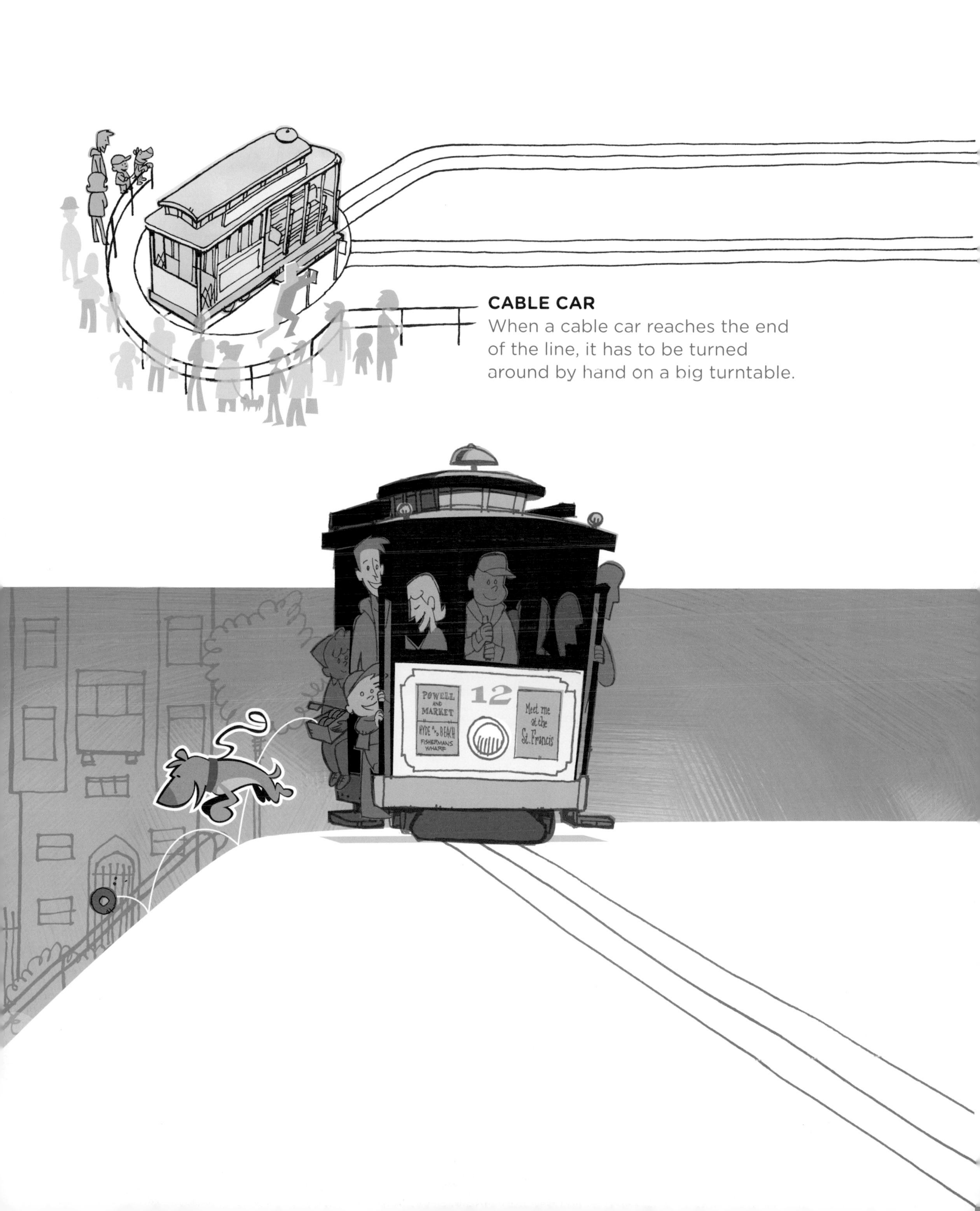

CABLE CAR
When a cable car reaches the end of the line, it has to be turned around by hand on a big turntable.

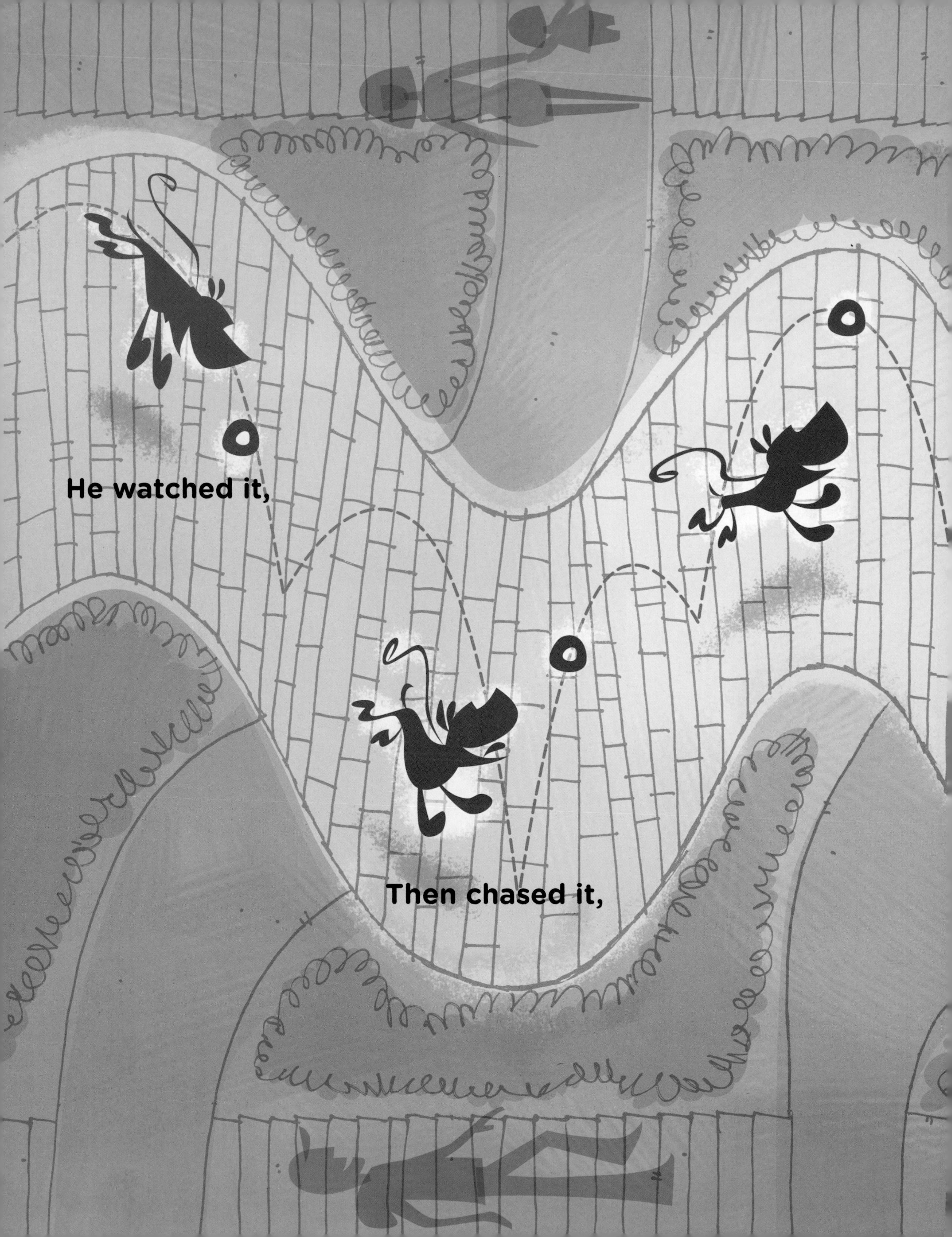

He watched it,

Then chased it,

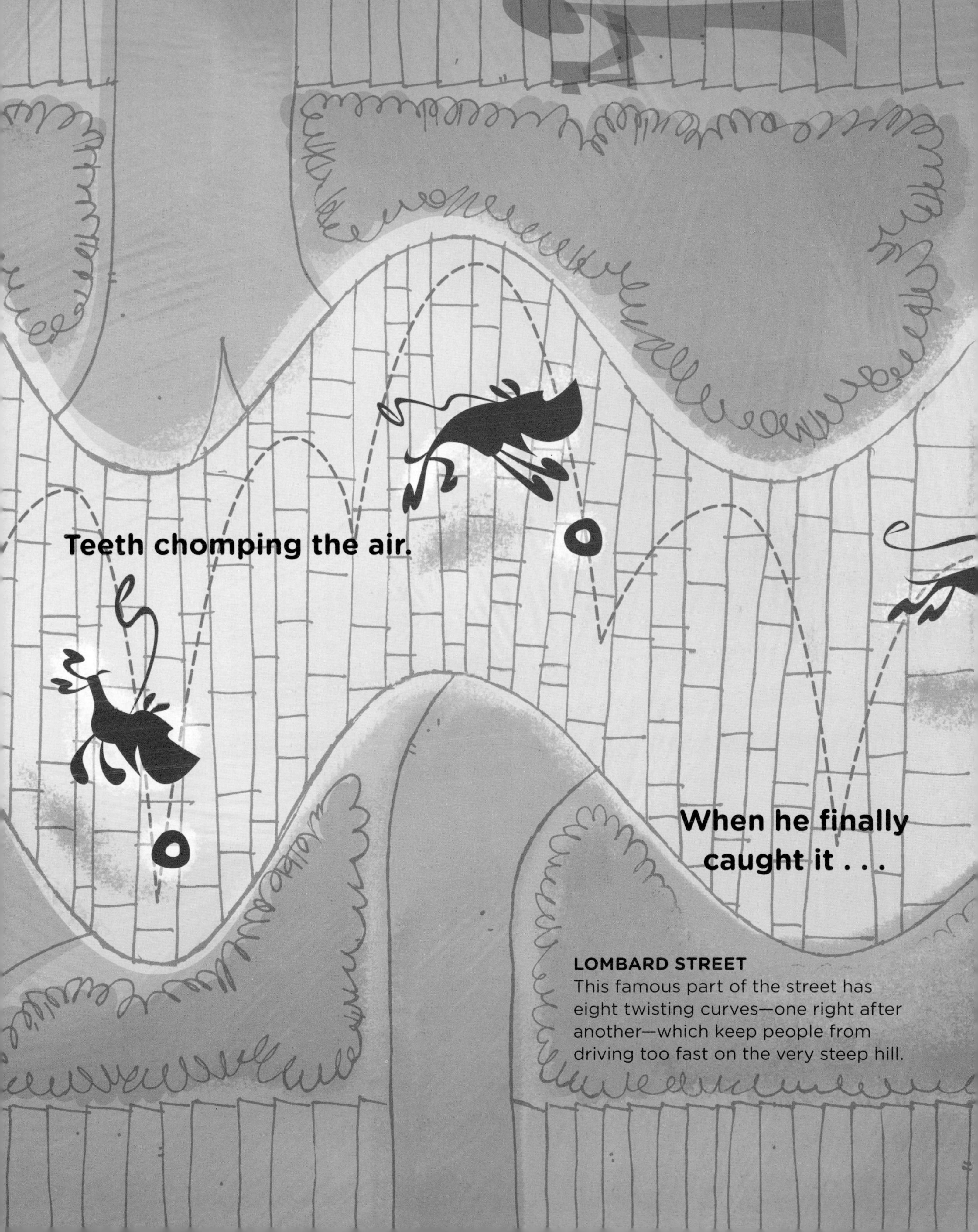

Teeth chomping the air.

When he finally caught it . . .

LOMBARD STREET

This famous part of the street has eight twisting curves—one right after another—which keep people from driving too fast on the very steep hill.

Pete wasn't there!

Larry suddenly felt an
"Uh-oh" in his heart.
He had to find Pete,
But where should he start?

Running, not knowing
Which way he should take,
He searched through
A neighborhood
That was colored like cake.

ALAMO SQUARE
This park is the home of the famous row of Victorian houses known as "The Painted Ladies" or "The Six Sisters."

Higher and higher
Ran the lost little pup.
Up a hill. Up a tower.
Up . . . **UP . . . UP!**

But even from here
He could not see his friend,
So to search somewhere else,
He ran back down again.

COIT TOWER
At the very top of Telegraph Hill, from Coit Tower you can see all of San Francisco.

He then found himself
at a fisherman's place.
Streetcars brought people
who shopped at fast pace.

He rode on a ferry
To an island of rock
Where many small rooms
Each had bars and a lock.

An interesting visit,
But who'd want to stay.
Larry was happy
To ferry away.

FISHERMAN'S WHARF
This is the place San Francisco's fishing boats call home, but now the wharf is more famous for its shops and seafood restaurants.

ALCATRAZ ISLAND
Nicknamed "The Rock," this island has been home to a lighthouse, a military fort, and a prison. Now the National Park Service gives tours.

High up in an elevator made out of glass,
Larry looked down and saw lots of folks pass.

Far below, in the crowd on the bustling street
He checked every person . . .
But couldn't see Pete.

UNION SQUARE
The glass elevators on the outside of the St. Francis Hotel rise 32 stories above the street.

His search took him next to a big, noisy place,
Part museum, part factory, inside the same space.

The cables come in and go out underground,
Pulling the cable cars all over town!

CABLE CAR MUSEUM
Here, visitors can see antique cable cars and watch the giant wheels turn as they pull the cable cars up and down the city's steep streets.

He then met some lions
Whose faces were stone
And he asked them to help him
Be not so alone.

They offered no answer.
Larry did not want to wait,
So he left them to stand
Watchful guard at their gate.

DRAGON GATE
The Chinese call the two stone lions that guard this gate "foo dogs."

Just past the gate some strange buildings appeared.
New smells reached his nose. New sounds filled his ears.

In the crowded confusion he saw one restaurant spot
That could stop passersby whether hungry or not.

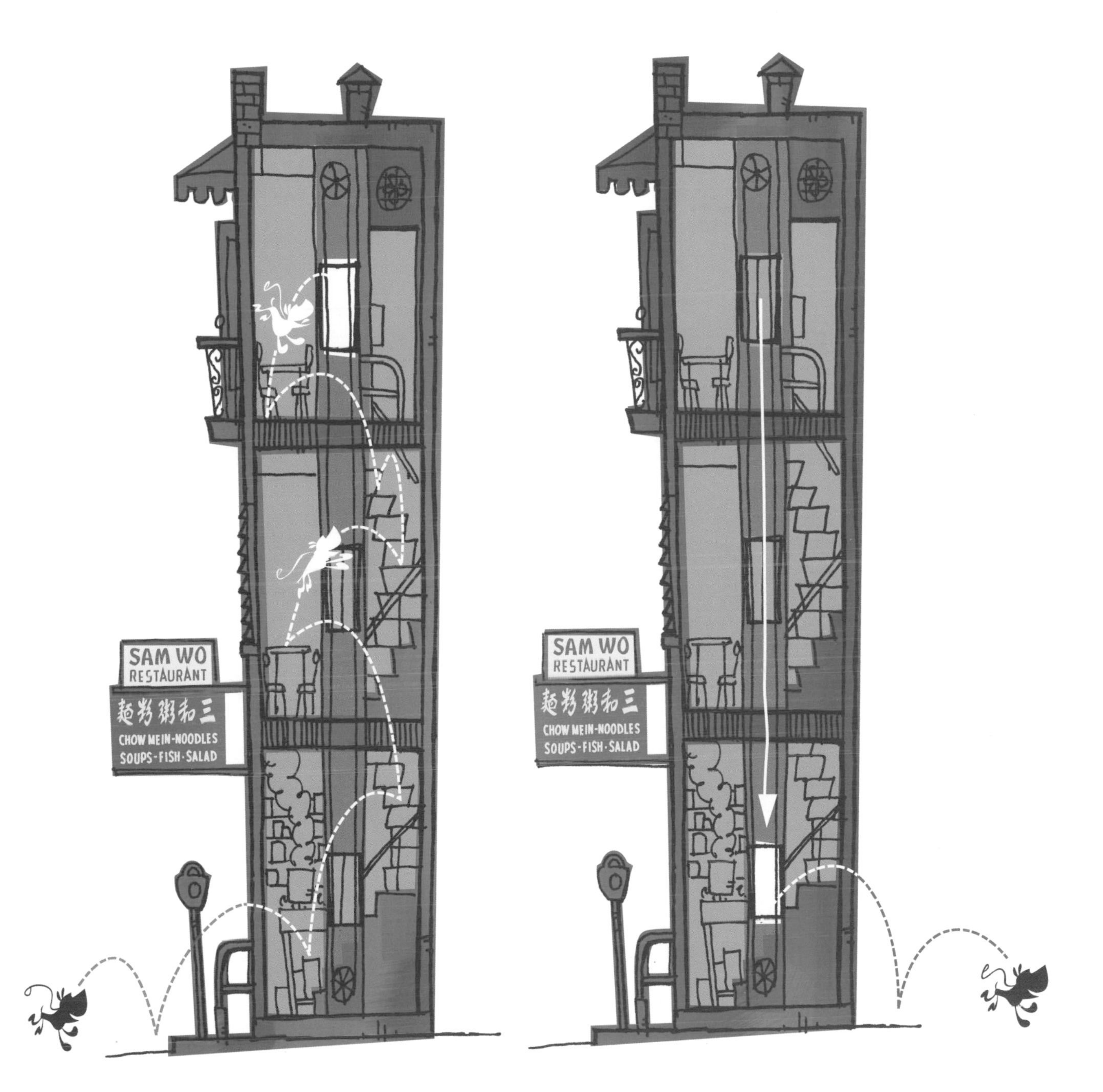

SAM WO'S
This 100-year-old restaurant has a tiny elevator, which is used to send food from the kitchen to the upstairs dining room.

He saw a huge arrow stuck into the ground
As if some giant archer left it there to be found.

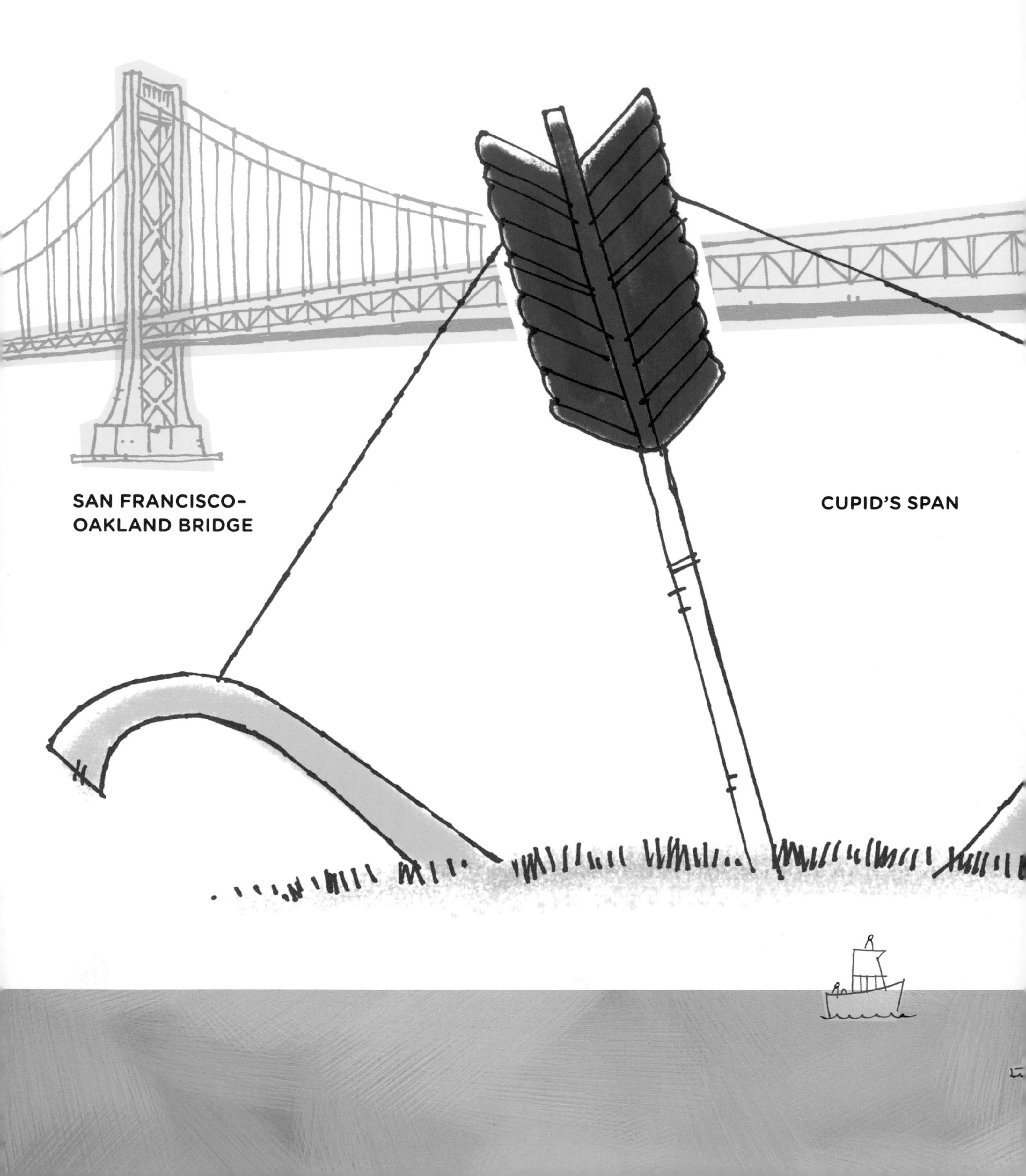

And speaking of Giants, around here they play ball.
A loud cheer made everyone outside watch a wall.

To see this with Pete our friend Larry was wishing,
While people in boats did a strange kind of fishing.

AT&T PARK
When home runs are hit out of the park into the bay, they're called "splash hits."

JAPANESE TEA GARDEN

This is the oldest public Japanese garden in the United States, built in 1894.
The Drum Bridge is so steep that there are steps you must climb like a ladder.
Its reflection in the water makes a circle.

He discovered a place
Not so "city" at all.
There were bonsais and rocks
Near a small waterfall.

If he'd been there with Pete,
He'd be happy to stay,
But he wasn't done looking,
So Larry went on his way.

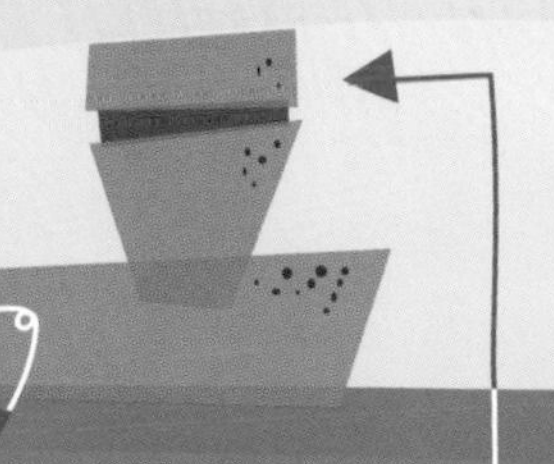

M. H. DE YOUNG MUSEUM
This fine arts museum has a 9-story observation tower that gives you a view of the whole park.

MISSION DOLORES
The oldest building in San Francisco,
the mission was founded in June of 1776.

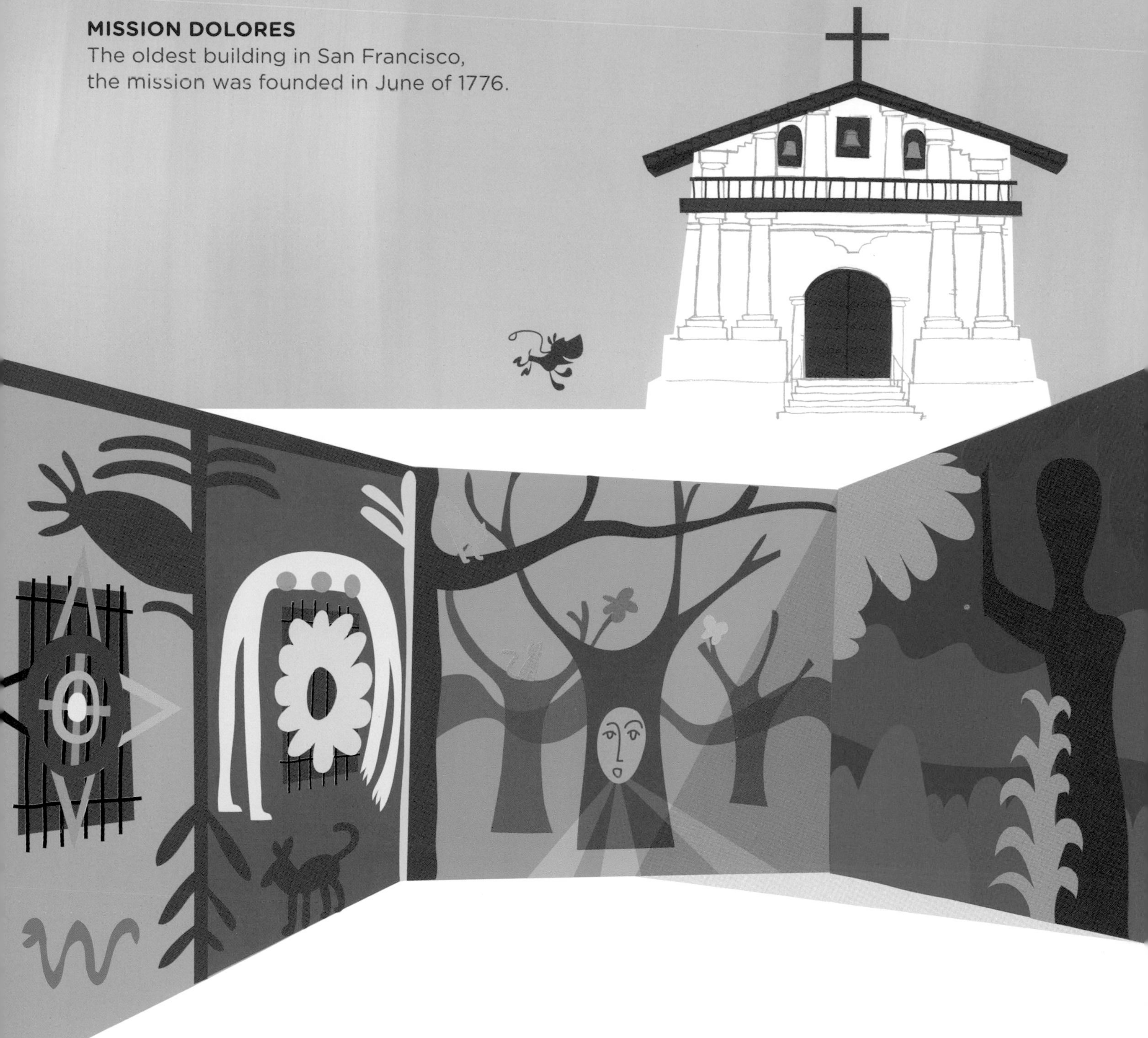

Some streets in this place looked like museum halls,
With huge paintings painted on fences and walls.

There were portraits and all kinds of interesting scenes
Brought to life through **reds, yellows, purples,** and **greens.**

MISSION DISTRICT

A young man with paint splotches
All over his clothes
Looked down to see
Larry right under his nose.

He smiled at Larry and asked,
"Are you alone?"
Then he checked the dog's collar
And took out his phone.

SEAL ROCK
Here is where
San Francisco
meets the
Pacific Ocean.

The artist knew lots
About helping lost pets.
He found Pete at the place
That's as "coast" as it gets.

Larry jumped up
And wagged his tail,
Licking Pete's face,
And they stood there,
Locked in a big embrace.

Pete shared with Larry the things he had seen,
And wondered out loud just where Larry had been.

Then they fell fast asleep as the car drove away.
It had been quite an adventurous day.

Get More Out of This Book

A Diverse Community

San Francisco has a significant Asian and Asian-American population, particularly people of Chinese and Japanese descent. Chinatown in San Francisco is the oldest in North America and home to the largest Chinese community outside of Asia. Choose a Chinese or Japanese folktale to read aloud. Have a selection of picture books with Asian and Asian-American characters available for browsing.

Time to Rhyme

The cable cars are one of San Francisco's most famous attractions. Re-read aloud the rhyme about when Pete and Larry are boarding:

Pete's parents reminded them, "Don't wander far"
As they excitedly boarded a cable car.
These vehicles pulled along tracks on the ground
Are a popular way to get around town.
For the ride Larry sat himself right beside Pete
'Til he saw a glazed donut roll by down the street.

See if readers can come up with five more rhyming words for each of the couplets: rhymes with far/car; ground/town; Pete/street. Later in the book, Larry runs through the Cable Car Museum. Readers can visit their website at CableCarMuseum.org to find out more.

Good as Gold

The Golden Gate Bridge is one of the most famous bridges in the world. Ask readers to imagine that they are a worker who has been asked to fix something at the very top of the bridge. Just suppose that it was a clear day with no fog (unusual in San Francisco!)—have readers write or dictate what their view is like. Can they see the Bay Bridge? Mountains? The ocean? Chinatown?

TEACHER'S GUIDE: The above discussion questions and activities are from our teacher's guide, which is aligned to the Common Core State Standards for English Language Arts for Grades K to 1. For the complete guide and a list of the exact standards it aligns with, visit our website: SasquatchBooks.com